The Bizarre Hockey Tournament

The Bizarre
Hockey Tournament

by

Jerry B. Jenkins

MOODY PRESS
CHICAGO

ISBN: 0-8024-8236-8

2 3 4 5 6 Printing/LC/Year 90 89 88 87 86

Printed in the United States of America

To Arthur Taylor

Contents

1
Goalie Tryouts

As I sat there watching the first preliminary round game, I knew the Baker Street Sports Club didn't belong in the state hockey tournament. No one needed to tell me that. I was captain of the team; I knew better than anyone else that we'd been lucky.

Lucky? That was hardly the word for it. Just to put six players on the ice, our club had to raise hundreds and hundreds of dollars. It wasn't long—I'd say about three and a half minutes into our first real game of the season—before we realized that six players were hardly enough.

A hockey team is made up of six players at a time, we knew. But we didn't realize that most teams switch their offensive lines every few minutes. We quickly found out why. We were dead tired, exhausted, beat.

That made me wish we'd worked just a little harder, stayed at it a little longer, and raised enough money for equipment for a couple more of the guys. It hadn't been easy to decide who would get to play and who wouldn't. We thought about trading off, some guys playing one game and others the next, but that just wouldn't have worked.

I was proud of those members of the club who volunteered

to let others play—and then still jumped into the money raising activities with just as much enthusiasm. It takes a good kid to do that. We were mowing lawns all summer between baseball games and raking leaves all fall between football and basketball games.

We finally got enough money for the goalie's equipment. That was the most expensive, with the extra padding and the face mask and all. Then we had to figure out who would be goalie. Just as many of the guys *didn't* want to as did, so that helped. I always thought big Jack Bastable would be our goalie, but we had finally found a game at which Jack didn't excel.

He was bigger than the average twelve-year-old and was retarded, but he was also one of the best athletes I ever saw. For sure he was the top basketball player of his age anywhere, and he played a good game of football and soccer too. But he couldn't skate—and couldn't learn. Not that he didn't try for several weeks. We still wanted him involved, of course, because he had the sweetest and most cooperative spirit of anyone in our club, so we made him our equipment manager.

Toby, a big, slow running kid; Cory, our fiery redhead; and Jimmy, thick, dark haired, and my best friend, wound up competing for the goalie position. Remember, this was before we had any of the other equipment.

We couldn't wait until the pond froze over, and we weren't allowed into the local rink without proper equipment for everyone and all our registration fees paid, so we played "ice" hockey right on Baker Street.

There was hardly ever any traffic there, so we rigged up a goal from various pieces of corrugated steel roofing. The pucks and sticks were the cheapest things for us to buy, but we ruined our sticks the first few days by playing on asphalt. We just scraped the stick blades down to sawdust.

But did we ever have fun. We helped Toby get suited up first. He looked funny inside all that bulky gear, but we knew it was necessary. He was in sneakers because we didn't want

4

him ruining the expensive goalie skates. But besides that, he was decked out just as any goalie would be for a real game on the ice.

He had the gigantic shin guards that formed a big square when he put his knees together, and there was enough padding elsewhere for his thighs and arms and shoulders. He had a helmet and a face mask on, but we could see right through the holes to his embarrassed expression. We knew he was praying no cars would come along.

He looked like something from outer space, and we got some good laughs out of it. But he kept threatening us by waving his leather gloves at us and telling us to get on with it. "I'm gonna be the best goalie, so good you won't even want the other buys to try out. C'mon! C'mon!"

I was still chuckling as I dug three fresh, new, hard rubber pucks from their little boxes and motioned for the guys with sticks to line up about thirty feet from Toby and the jerry-rigged goal mouth.

"Just a minute, Tob'! Let me see what kinda sound it's gonna make if one does happen to get past you."

He didn't move. "C'mon, O'Neil! Nothin's gonna get past me anyway!"

I waved him aside. "Just move, Toby. I just wanna get the feel of it."

He trudged off to the side, and I lined up a shot. None of us was really new to the game. We'd been playing hockey on the frozen pond for years, but all we had were hand-me-down skates and cheap sticks before. No padding, helmets, face masks, or anything. Jimmy wore a football helmet with a faceguard cage on it when he was in the goal, but that was all the "equipment" we had ever used before.

Now that we wanted to join a real league, it would cost more than two hundred dollars per player for equipment alone.

I jockeyed the puck back and forth with my stick and was troubled that it wouldn't cooperate on the pavement. I

5

backhanded it over to Bugsy, our black club member. "Feed me, Bugs. Maybe that'll work."

He was smooth and fluid as always and drew his stick back to cushion the smack of the puck against it. He crouched into a passing stance and softly slid it to me. Just as it reached the point where I would reach out and accept it, then shoot, the warm hunk of rubber rolled up on its side, spun in a circle, and seemed to stagger away from me like a drunk mouse.

The guys were doubling over from laughing, and I suddenly knew how Toby felt, standing there sweating in the equipment and wishing we would quit horsing around and get on with it. I hustled after the puck, set it before me, and tried a lefthanded slap shot from about twenty-five feet away from the corrugated steel "goal."

The puck slid straight for ten feet, turned up on its side, bounced once, then floated about ten feet over the goal. Now it was Toby's turn to laugh. He chased after the puck, calling over his shoulder. "Maybe you shoulda froze the puck first, the way they do when you play on ice! I'm gettin' in the crease, and you guys can start shootin'! That is, if any of ya think you can come close, let alone get it past me!"

He retrieved the puck and tossed it out to the guys in line. Jimmy was up first. He had a look in his eye, but I had no idea what was on his mind. He set the puck to his left, the way I had, but he was farther back. He pretended to sweep at it with his stick, but lifted the blade at the last instant, dropped his stick, and ran around the puck.

He picked it up in his right hand, like a catcher grabbing a bunt, and fired it directly at Toby. Jimmy had always been big and strong and could throw hard, but we'd never seen him throw a puck before. It caught the wind and swept from left to right, right in front of Toby.

The big goalie was yelling something as he half tried to get out of the way and half tried to catch it with his left glove. The puck darted just out of his reach and slammed against the

6

steel. *Thwang!!!* It was so loud we almost had to cover our ears.

Jimmy grinned. "You wanted to know what it would sound like, Dal! That's what it sounds like! I knew I couldn't shoot it in from here if you couldn't from there."

We were all laughing and shaking our heads at the incredible noise it had made. There would certainly be no doubt when a goal was scored!

Toby was mad. "You guys gonna give me a tryout or not? Maybe you all wanna just come up here and throw the stinkin' puck against the metal, huh? You gonna name me goalie, Dallas, or are we gonna have tryouts here?"

I got serious. "All right. Everybody with a stick get in line. Shoot the best you can from out there, and Toby will toss the pucks back."

It wasn't long before we had caught on to how to best shoot a puck outside on dry ground. Soon we were launching shots that stayed about six inches off the ground until they reached Toby. Then they would bounce in front of his feet, and he would dance to either get out of the way or try to block them with his stick or catch them.

Brent got off the best early shot. He stepped up a couple of feet, switched the puck from his left to his right, and backhanded a shot that hugged the ground the whole way toward the goal.

Toby kept expecting it to start hopping and jumping as usual, or maybe roll away as most of them did. But this was a good shot.

It continued straight toward him. He was so prepared for the awkward angle, or sudden change of direction that never came, that he wasn't prepared for the shot to head straight into the goal as if it had been planned that way.

Toby had stood ready to move one way or the other, and his hands spread at the last instant as the puck flew past untouched. It clanged off the goal with a resounding echo, and

Brent raised his arms the way the pros do when they've scored. The rest of us danced around him and poked him with our sticks and clapped him on the back. The only thing missing was our equipment and the ice.

Toby was doing his best, but his temper made him fail more than he succeeded. Once, when a shot by Cory bounced between his legs and slammed off the metal goal, Toby turned around and swept at the puck with his stick, banging the metal.

He whirled to tell us that that was not another goal but just his stick, but that threw him off balance. As he tried to stay on his feet, his stick hit the metal yet again.

Cory was hysterical. "Three goals in one shot!"

But Toby was going down. He stepped backward with short choppy steps, trying to keep his balance, and found himself perched atop the low strip of metal. As he went over backward, his elbows banged the goal and so did his heels and the back of his helmet. It sounded like World War III, and we couldn't keep from laughing.

Toby went head over heels, and the metal goal flopped back over him, banging and clanging, the dust rising. Even he couldn't keep from laughing. He muttered, "I think I've had enough."

And we laughed till we cried.

2

Breaking the News

Toby enjoyed firing shots at Cory when Cory was suited up in the goalie gear. In fact, Toby thought that was pretty special. Unfortunately, he wasn't much better as a shooter than he had been as a goalie, but I remembered from the previous winter that he was a good skater and tough on the ice.

That meant that Toby, while he couldn't shoot or play goalie, could start for the Baker Street Sports Club hockey team as a defenseman. I saw him as right defenseman, and while I hadn't checked that out with the rest of the guys as I usually did, I knew I had one position nailed down.

Cory was good in the net, even though ours didn't have any mesh like a real net. He was surprisingly quick and able to get to most of the shots. The problem was, we didn't figure anyone his size would be interested in the position.

So the uniform and the gear overwhelmed him and hung almost to the ground. The shots that came to him or near him, he caught or batted away. But the ones a foot away or more slipped past him and clanged off our makeshift goal.

He wanted the goalie position, I could tell. He worked hard

at it, looked even more determined when a shot got past him, and looked proud and content when he blocked shots. Even Toby grudgingly agreed. "He's good. Man, he's good."

When it was time for Jimmy to try out, Cory took the equipment off slowly, a look of satisfaction on his face. He wished Jimmy luck, sincerely yet almost as if he thought the big guy didn't have a chance.

I thought Cory must have a short memory. Jimmy had always played goalie on the pond. He was quick and agile and coordinated for a big guy, and he seemed to have a sixth sense for where the puck would be. Even when his vision was blocked by his own defensemen, he somehow knew.

He was big enough to fill up a good portion of the goal mouth, which was a big advantage over Cory, who was strong and wiry but didn't have the bulk.

Jimmy looked like he belonged in the net. Ten or twelve shots were fired before one got past him. He hunched low, his big, squared off goalie stick dragging along the pavement. He prowled back and forth before the goal like a great cat protecting its home.

Only Cory could score on him, but then Cory wanted to prove he was the best goalie. I shot three straight slapshots to the corners of the goal, but Jimmy turned them back, twice making them roll right to me again. That was a mistake, because I was wound up and ready to shoot again. Still, I couldn't penetrate the goal.

Cory scored on a neat slip backhand and a charging, hand-switching drive. The puck bounced off Jimmy's glove, and he called out a compliment as it gonged off the metal. "Nice shot, Cor'!"

Cory just grimaced and kept shooting, scoring again. If he thought he had convinced me that he was the best goalie, he was mistaken. Jimmy was clearly better, the only choice. The gear fit him best, he was more at home in the net, and he would be my man.

12

He was also encouraging to his teammates. I mean, to compliment one of your rivals on a shot that got past you, well, that was a new Jimmy. Ever since he had become a Christian and was going to church and Sunday school with me every Sunday, his attitude had changed.

The same was true with Cory, but we three were the only Christians in the club. Cory still had trouble with his temper and with sulking, but he was easier to talk to now. I didn't look forward to breaking the news to him about Jimmy's being my choice as goalie, but I knew I would have to face it. I had good news for him too, but I wasn't sure he wanted to hear it.

Brent and Bugsy and I were the other three best skaters and shooters, so I pretty much had my team. I first called around all the guys who weren't going to make it and asked them to meet me at the shed in the back of our property.

"I know you guys all wanted to be on the team, and I want you to know that if anybody gets hurt, I'll be coming back to you for another tryout. But we've only got enough equipment ordered for the six who are going to be starting, and I know none of you can afford stuff on your own. Thanks for understanding, for helping raise money, and for supporting the club even though you can't play this season."

They were great. Nobody complained. No one was really surprised. They were good in other sports, and they would stay with the club, cheering us on. They were all young and mostly little, and they knew that their day would come soon enough.

Then I talked alone to each of the ones who made it.

"Bugsy, I want you to play left defenseman. You can still shoot and score from that position, but you're so agile and skate backward so well, I think you'll be best there."

He was pleased.

I told Brent that I would let him choose between left wing or center on the offensive line and that I would take the other.

13

"Oh, I couldn't play center, Dallas, I'm not big enough. I've got the speed, yeah, but you should play center. I'll get ahead near the blue line, and you can lead me with passes. Who's going to be on the other wing?"

"I may be."

"I thought you said you'd take center if I wanted left wing."

"Yeah, but I'm gonna make the same offer to the other guy on the line. I'll let you know as soon as I've talked with him."

I sat with Toby on my back porch and told him I thought he could help the team most by playing right defenseman. He sat sadly shaking his head. "I knew Cory beat me out for goalie."

"You did, huh?"

"Yeah. It was obvious."

"It wasn't obvious to me, Tob'."

"You mean I almost beat him out?"

"I didn't say that. I just said it wasn't that obvious to me. Now, are you satisfied to do a good job for us as a defenseman? You'll be teamed up with Bugsy. He'll be on the other side."

"Sure, Dallas. I'm glad to have made the team. I don't have to hang around the goal all the time, do I? I mean the way the fullbacks usually do in soccer?"

"Nah! In hockey some of the highest scorers are defensemen. When we've got the puck down at the other end of the ice, I'll want you down there with us, working the plays. If the puck gets stolen, we all have to hustle back, huh?"

He nodded and smiled. "I can hustle with skates on. Running isn't my thing, but I can move pretty well on the ice."

"I know. I'll be countin' on you to help us a lot this year, Toby."

Only Jimmy and Cory were waiting in the darkness, sitting in the dewy grass in our backyard. I called for Jimmy. He ambled over while Cory sat toying with the goalie equipment. I talked softly so Cory wouldn't hear and be disappointed in advance.

"Jimmy, I want you to be goalie and to take the equipment home. Get used to it, adjust it, make sure the leather is toned and treated. OK?"

He smiled and nodded but knew enough to whisper. "Is Cory going to be upset?"

"I suppose. But I have to do what's best for the team."

"I wasn't sure you would, Dal."

"What do you mean? Don't I always?"

"Yeah, I don't mean that. I mean, I thought maybe you'd think that Cory in the goal would be better for the team."

I shook my head. "No, it was clear you were best. Wasn't it to you?"

"Not really. Cory was pretty quick."

"But too small."

Jimmy shrugged. "Well, I'm glad anyway. I'll do my best. I just hope Cory doesn't get mad at you, or me, or the rest of the club."

"He shouldn't."

"I know he shouldn't, but he usually does."

"Not since he's become a Christian."

"Yeah, but he's still got a temper. Listen, should I take the equipment right away? I mean, then he'll know even before you tell him. In fact, he probably already knows by looking at me and seeing that I'm not disappointed."

I thought a moment. "You're probably right. Just go ahead and take it. It'll be all right. Listen, there's another reason I'm putting Cory somewhere else on the team."

"Yeah? What?"

"Well, I guess I'd better tell him first, don't you think?"

Jimmy looked exasperated. "Why'd you start to tell me then?"

"I'm sorry."

He shook his head, shrugged, and ambled off the porch toward Cory. "Dal wants you."

Cory rose, then turned to see Jimmy gathering up the gear. The energy drained from Cory's body, and he moved toward

15

me like an old man on his last legs.

He hunkered down on the step below me and sat with his back to me so that when he did speak, I could hardly hear him. "Bad news, huh?"

"Depends."

"On what?"

"On how you take it. You made the team, you know."

"I figured that."

"But you had counted on being the goalie."

"I was the best in the goal, Dallas."

"I didn't think so, but I did think you were better somewhere else."

"Better than who?"

"Better than all of us."

"You kidding?"

I shook my head. "Nope."

"Where?"

"Offensive line. You can be center or right wing. You decide."

"You *are* kidding."

"I'm not. You had one of the best shots out there. More accurate more often. And I know how you skate. You'll be good for us."

He turned and looked up at me. "I really wanted to be goalie, Dallas."

I nodded. "I know. But Jimmy was better there, in my opinion. And choosing the lineup is what I'm supposed to do."

"I'm not arguing that, Dallas. I'm just disappointed."

"Disappointed at making the starting lineup and getting to choose your position?"

"If I get to choose, I'll choose goalie."

"You get to choose between center and right wing on the offensive line. I need a guy who can stickhandle, control the puck, pass, and shoot."

"Yeah? And what're *you* gonna play—defenseman?"

16

"I'll play whatever you don't play."

"Then you'll be playing center *and* right wing, Dallas. Because I'm not playing."

3

The Blowup

At first I thought Cory had thrown out that remark just so
we could talk about it, but it wasn't long before I realized
he was serious. He stood and walked toward his bike, and by
the time I figured out that he was actually leaving, his
headlight was on.

"Cory! C'mon, man! What's the problem? We're friends.
You can talk to me."

I bounded off the porch and hurried over to him, hoping he
wouldn't just ride away. When I got to him I noticed in the
darkness that he was just straddling his bike, going nowhere.

He sighed. "I guess it isn't that I really thought I was a better goalie than Jimmy. He was good. Smooth. Natural. He
belongs there. But I don't want to play anywhere else."

"Why not?"

"I don't know if I want to talk about it."

"Cory, I've seen you skate. You're a tough player. A good
shooter. A good passer. A hard checker." He winced, and I
knew I had hit upon a sore spot. "What? You don't like to
check people hard?" I punched him lightly on the shoulder.
"Good ol' tough guy Cory?"

He wasn't smiling. I shook my head. What had gotten into

him? Cory had always loved a good clean scrap as much as anyone. And in hockey, a solid check was all part of the game, just like a block or a tackle in football.

When he finally spoke, it was just above a whisper, as if he'd rather have just ridden off and burst into tears. "I think it has somethin' to do with my becoming a Christian."

I nodded. "You're wondering if Jesus would want you smashin' into guys, tryin' to make them lose the puck?"

He nodded. "I know it's all part of the game, and there are legal and illegal ways of doing it, but when we played on the pond, all we did was argue about whether a guy took too many steps before hitting the other player and all that. Then it would end up in fistfights."

I knew what he meant. There had been plenty of those, and Cory had usually been in the middle of them. Still, I did my best to reason with him. "It didn't have to end up in a fight. I never fought."

"That's just it, Dallas. Don't you see? We all figured you didn't fight because you were a church kid and a nice guy. Now I know it was more than that. I know it was that you were a Christian and that Jesus was part of your life. Well, that's true for me now too, so I wouldn't be fighting."

"There you go. So what's the problem? You won't fight, but you'll play the game good and hard like I do, follow the rules, pray that God will keep your temper under control, and enjoy hockey."

"I could enjoy it from the goal, but not out on the open ice. I've still got my temper, and even if a guy got a clean shot on me, I'd want to get back at him. I just know I would."

I had to think about that one for a while. Finally, I spoke. "So, is that going to be your solution? For the rest of your life, in order to live the way you think God wants you to, you're going to run from every situation that might make you fail?"

Cory nodded. "I'm not sure you should try to make that sound so stupid, Dallas. We're supposed to flee the devil and abstain from all appearance of evil. What's wrong with turning tail and running from situations we know we can't handle?"

"Nothing. Unless it's a situation you should *learn* to handle. Why rob yourself of the pleasure of playing hockey just because you think you'll get in God's way on the ice? Can't He keep you from sinning?"

"Maybe someday, but I still battle this temper, Dal."

"I know, and I think you've come a long way."

"I *have!* And I don't want to blow it now."

"Well, I wish you'd give it a try. Jimmy and I can pray for you every minute you're on the ice. And if you feel yourself getting too angry or wanting to get back at someone, just let us know and we'll step in and cool you down."

Cory looked as if he wanted to think about that. A few days later he told me he was willing to try.

Not long after that, all of our gear and uniforms arrived. I thought the hockey uniforms were as handsome as any the Baker Street Sports Club had owned for any sport.

Our skates were reinforced to protect our ankles and our achilles tendons. The socks were white with blue and red stripes around the calves. The bulky shorts fit over all our padding and were solid blue with a wide red vertical stripe with white piping and a blue, lower-case B at the bottom of each side.

The jerseys were long sleeved and solid blue with our numbers on the back and on the left arm below the shoulder, white in a wide red stripe. Our helmets were navy, and our gloves were navy and red to match the uniforms.

Usually our rule was that we never used our uniforms except during games, but we didn't really have practice uniforms, and with all the padding on we needed the uniforms. Plus we needed to get used to the whole package, so we changed our rules.

We practiced on the pond until we could get into the rink, and we felt special. We felt good and looked good and our play seemed to improve overnight. I talked and talked about

21

the importance of teamwork, and we drilled on passing, shooting, checking, skating, knowing where everyone was at all times, and playing defense.

The problem was, we wouldn't really know how good we were until we got some real competition.

The first bit of trouble Cory got into was with Toby. The big guy was still a little miffed that he wasn't the goalie, and so he played defense particularly hard. He wanted to shoot and help the offense, and I reminded him that there would be plenty of time for that. Meanwhile, I needed him to play hard defense with Bugsy and Jimmy against Brent and Cory and me.

And he was ready.

I instructed the defense to get into position while I put rags at the edges of the pond to mark the attack zone blue line. The offense called itself offside the first couple of times up the ice, and it was clear the defense was getting restless.

Toby started muttering and complaining and finally yelling about being bored.

I tried to take control. "All right! This time we're going to rush the goal and work our play even if we're a little offside! Let's go!"

Brent popped the puck past me to Cory on the right wing, and I hustled to get ahead of my two teammates because the play called for me to cut back at the blue line and lead whichever one of them was open.

Cory slightly mishandled the puck, and I knew I was closer to the blue line than I wanted to be when I scraped to a stop. I didn't think I was offside yet, but suddenly Cory regained control of the puck and passed it directly back to me. In dancing around to receive his pass, I may have stepped over the line, but the plan was that we continue anyway.

Meanwhile, Brent thought I would be leading him, since he was open. My only hope was to take the puck into the zone myself and hope I was still ahead of my wings.

Of course, no one on the defense thought I was, and all three began to shout. "Offside!"

"I know. Let's finish the play!"

Even Jimmy was yelling. "But you're all three offside! All three of you!"

Cory and Brent were crossing in front of me when I finally gave up. "All right! Offside! We'll start over!"

But only Brent heard me. Cory was digging hard to get into position and was puzzled when Toby—who had heard me—straightened up and relaxed. Cory turned to look at me, and when he saw I had ended the play, he stood up and glided past Toby.

Almost.

At the last instant, Toby drove his hip into Cory and sent him flying through the air, "Dead play, deaf man!"

Cory went down, his helmeted head banging the ice before he bounced back up to a sitting position, spinning on his seat, his stick sliding off the ice. He didn't appear to be hurt. He leaped to his feet, his face crimson. "You—!"

I motioned to Jimmy, who burst from the goal and skated directly over to Cory. He had dropped his stick and both goalie gloves and wrapped his arms around the redhead. "It's OK, man, it's OK. Dallas'll deal with it. Stay cool."

"He smashed me down for no reason!"

"It's all right, Cor'. Be cool."

Toby made a move to get closer to Cory, as if he wanted some more action. He tore off his helmet and swung it menacingly.

I had had it. "Toby! That's enough! That was uncalled for, and if I was a ref I'd have whistled you for a misconduct! This is your teammate, man! How are we going to develop any team spirit around here with that kind of garbage going on?"

He looked down and muttered. "I was just playin' around."

"Well, that's not the way we play around. I think you owe him an apology."

23

He looked at me defiantly. "If you think he's owed one, why don't you give him one?"

I stared at Toby in disbelief. That he would say something like that in front of the rest of the team and Jack was just amazing. "Come over here, Toby." I motioned for him to follow me.

I skated to the edge of the pond where some cattails were frozen into the ice. "I'm going to give you one chance to apologize to me for what you just said. Then you can apologize to your teammates. Then you can apologize to Cory. You know he has a temper, and he's working on it. He doesn't need this right now."

Toby glared at me. "I'll think about it."

"You'd better think fast, because you're not playing, you're not even practicing with this team until you do it. If you're not ready to do it right now, you can just sit and watch. Let me know when you're ready."

I glided back to the center of the ice where everyone was milling about. Cory seemed to have cooled down, so I called another play, and we regrouped at our end. Jimmy got his stuff back on and backed into the goal. But he was puzzled. "This a power play? Three on two?"

I stared at him, hoping he'd realize that I needed his support more than ever just then. He caught on quickly, and while he was using the same words, they had a different tone this time.

"OK! Power play drill! Three on two! Let's hold 'em!"

Toby sat glumly next to Jack Bastable, staring at the ground and not saying anything.

4

The New Surface

For some reason—maybe it was knowing that we had the defense outnumbered—our next play went off perfectly. That doesn't mean we scored a goal, because we didn't. But in hockey, a successful play is one in which you outsmart or outskate or overpower your opponent and get a decent shot on goal.

There are too many things that have too much to do with luck to feel bad about not scoring everytime you make a successful rush. The defense can get lucky. The goalie can be superb. The shot can be miscalculated, rushed, or delayed. Still, the basic play can be a success because you learn something.

You learn how to penetrate the defense, how to attack, how to get clear for a shot. And the more good shots you take, the more goals you eventually score. Luck eventually turns your way; the law of averages catches up with you. Our plan was to get off a good shot, and that we did.

We lined up as usual, Brent to my left, Cory to my right. Brent had the puck and let Cory get twenty feet ahead of him, me ten. We skated up the ice at that angle. Just before Cory got to the blue line, Brent appeared as if he were passing to me. Had I received the pass, Cory would have crossed the line before I could pass to him, but that was all part of the plan.

I let the pass go right through me to Cory, while the eyes of the defense were on me. The only defenseman besides the goalie, of course, was Bugsy, and he had his hands full. He skated toward me and then frantically back toward Cory. Cory centered the puck to me, and Bugsy lowered the boom on him.

Cory went down in a heap and slid off the ice, right past Jack and Toby. I was worried what might happen and whether Cory thought the check was legal and fair. From where I skated, it was.

I drove in toward the net with the puck, and Jimmy came out to meet me and cut down my angle. I dished the puck back to my left to Brent, who was streaking in at full speed. I rammed into Jimmy, and we both went down. The net was wide open for the left wing.

Brent carefully took aim and raised his stick. Only a miracle could stop the shot now. The miracle started with a B and ended with a Y. Bugsy had scrambled to his feet, apparently—at first—too late. He dove across the ice and stuck his stick out in front of him.

Brent's slapshot came up off the ice only an inch or so, not quite enough to get over Bugsy's stick. It grazed it, then flew over the goal. We all groaned, and then everyone congratulated everyone else on how well they had executed the play on both sides.

I whirled to find Cory. He was sitting next to Toby. It was clear that the big kid had already apologized. Cory was smiling and telling him it was all right. I skated over as Cory was leaving.

Toby looked up at me. "I'm sorry, Dallas. You were right. I shouldn't have done that."

I nodded and skated back to the ice. Toby followed and sounded sheepish as he called out. "Sorry, guys."

No one said anything, but we had a great practice after

that. In fact, we switched positions after a while and put Cory in the goal, while Brent and I played defensemen. I think the defense-turned-offense outscored us.

On one play, Toby lost his balance, tripped, and slid into the goal mouth, bringing Cory down on top of him. They both came up laughing, and I knew Cory was on his way. We would still have to see how he did in genuine competition.

I don't think any of us will ever forget our first practice on indoor ice. I know I never will. It was incredible. The rink was huge. We were directed to a goal at one end and told to stay out of everyone else's way.

There were little kids learning to figure skate at one end. In the middle a couple of coaches had their teams scrimmaging at three-quarter speed. And the other end, out to the blue line, was ours for an hour. We were told that after that, the entire rink would be ours for a half hour, and then the rink would be prepared for the first game of the league schedule. We would stay and watch that.

We thought the rink was noisy when we were just in the stands in our street clothes. The puck rattled off the boards and the shouts and sounds of the skate blades on the ice were nearly deafening. It was exciting, exhilarating.

We were nervous as we dressed in the locker room. There was no need to be, of course, because we were just going to skate around and get used to the ice. But to us, this was the big time. This was a privilege. Skating on ice that was frozen just for this purpose.

We giggled at each other and slapped each other on the back as we squeaked our way down the rubber matted hallway toward the rink. We pretended we were the U.S. olympic hockey team on its way out to the ice for the final match against the Russians.

Before we left home we had sharpened our skate blades, repaired our sticks, and gathered up all our pucks. While we were dressing, the pucks were in the rink freezer, getting solidified for proper use. They would roll and bounce less, the colder they were.

Jimmy carried all the pucks in his glove, and as we stepped out onto the rink, we all almost fell down. The plan was that we would simply skate around the perimeter of the area that had been assigned us, gliding around the back of the net, past the boards, and along the blue line.

We had learned to skate better than ever by carefully watching the pros, how they stayed in a low crouch and let their hips do most of the work. But the ice. We were not prepared for the ice.

The ice machine had been up and down the rink just a few minutes before we came out, so the ice was as fresh and flat and spotless as it could be. The ruts had been smoothed out, and the thin layer of fresh water had quickly hardened like glass. In our newly sharpened skates, we experienced skaters looked like pigs on the ice.

It was as if we had never skated before, as if our pond had been sandpaper. We were not used to the idea that our skate blades would not dig in, that we would not have to watch for little obstacles, that we would not have to learn where the soft spots, the indentations, the rough spots were.

We skated so much faster than ever! We would have looked at each other and said something, but we all faced the same sensation. It took all our intense concentration to keep from falling, and Jimmy nearly did. He took one lap, then grabbed the goal and nearly pulled it from the ice.

He dropped a half dozen pucks just inside the goal mouth and moved back and forth in the crease, preparing the ice for his brand of play. Meanwhile, the rest of us skated lap after lap, trying to get accustomed to the surface. What a treat it was. But what a frightening one.

And if we thought the sound was deafening from the stands, this was something else! I heard the sound of my blades on the ice as if it were being piped into my head through earphones. With my helmet on, I could hear my heartbeat, my breathing, and every other echoing sound in the rink.

Gradually, we got used to the noise and the surface, and we felt like supermen. I signaled everyone, offense and defense, to line up near the blue line. Jimmy knocked the pucks out to us. They came on a straight line, faster than he had intended. We each had to play goalie ourselves to keep them from getting into the scrimmage or, worse, tripping up a fledgling figure skater.

What we'd had to learn about skating on this surface, we had to learn about shooting as well. We had the feeling that the puck would travel faster than we were used to, but we had not figured how the very act of shooting could bring us down.

There simply wasn't the friction between ice and skate to lend balance the way we enjoyed it on the pond. A couple of the first guys to shoot went down quickly and were grateful for elbow pads and helmets.

I cautioned the guys to be careful, not just for their own sakes, but for Jimmy's as well. He wasn't used to seeing such fast shots, but we sure enjoyed launching them. Within a few minutes, I was aware of our mistake. We felt so good, so confident, so fresh on that surface that we considered ourselves pros.

We lined up and fired away, sending shots all over the boards and the plexiglass, and even a few into the goal. And each time Jimmy either dug one out and lobbed it back to us or one bounced off his pads, stick, or gloves and slid into our reach, we charged it and shot again.

I began to worry about Jimmy's stamina, but he seemed to be doing all right. I should have worried about everyone else's. It became obvious when one by one we began taking off our helmets briefly, just to let our heads cool. The steam rose off our hair as if we were on fire.

Our chests heaved with the effort to breathe, and I even noticed the pulse banging out in Bugsy's neck. We were huffing and puffing but not wanting to quit. Finally I called everyone around, and we wearily skated to the goal.

Jimmy was beaming as he pulled off his face mask. "This is somethin', huh?"

It sure was. But no one had the energy to respond. An official from the league, the one who had taken our registration check, walked to the end of the rink and motioned me over to the boards.

"You boys' first time on good ice?"

I nodded, smiling, unable to speak.

"I should have known. Wish I'd warned you to take it easy the first time. This is fairly common, you know. You boys'd better call it a night."

"Already? We just started, and we were kinda hoping we could scrimmage with one of the teams at center rink."

He shook his head. "Really, you shouldn't overdo it the first time."

"But we wanted to do a full rink drill when everyone else cleared out."

"You haven't got a guy who'd be able to do it now. Could *you*?"

I shook my head. He assured me there would be plenty of ice time for the Baker Street Sports Club. "You guys will get in shape."

Indeed we would.

5

The Season Begins

Four nights later we got our first taste of real competition. If it hadn't been for some good fortune early in the game, we'd have gone home shut out and dejected. As it was, we went home beaten 6-2 and somewhat encouraged.

That first night at the rink we had stayed around and watched the first league game. We were impressed. And scared. Both teams looked sharp and tough. The league was carefully officiated and coached, and any fighting resulted in immediate ejections from the game and—so we were told—suspensions from play for up to three games.

We hadn't noticed how often the teams changed players until our first game. Then we recalled that there had been a lot of switching in the first game we had watched. The team we played against, the Bay Side Bobcats, changed offensive lines every two minutes or so, and they even changed defensemen occasionally.

We had the same sensation on the ice when we skated out for the game that we had had the first night at the rink. We were over-eager, firing away at Jimmy and really making him work. This time, however, it didn't take us long to realize that we were making the same mistake as before.

We slowed down, saved some energy, and when the game started, we were ready. We were all nervous, and I was jittery when the puck came to me off the face-off. I should have looked up the ice and decided what I wanted to do, but all I could think of was all our friends and family in the stands and how everyone was watching us because we were a brand new team and the only one without an adult coach.

I wanted to get rid of the puck as soon as I could. I saw Cory streaking toward the blue line, but he was covered and I didn't think I could hit him with a pass. I sensed Brent on the left, skating free. I dished off a pass to him, hoping that Cory would slow down enough to let the puck and Brent get across the blue line first.

He did. But Brent was going so fast (and we were not really communicating with one another) that none of the three of us really knew what to do. We were so full of enthusiasm that we had quickly skated past the Bobcat defense and had the advantage.

But I wasn't ready for a return pass. Brent could see that. And Cory, though skating well, had fast been picked up by our opponent's best defender. He was still covered.

So there Brent was, with the puck, skating fast and clear into the attack zone but with little or no help from his teammates. Toby and Bugsy had followed us, and both were yelling at me to get in front of the net for the centering pass from Brent.

I hate to admit how confused I was. I simply had not expected us to win the face-off, let alone get before their net so quickly. I had been thinking defense and how to keep them from scoring for as long as possible in the hope that we could tire them out and catch them napping.

But we had done that from the opening face-off, and I, the captain and center, was messing up the play. My own defenders caught and passed me, and suddenly there was Bugsy in front of the net, looking for Brent's pass.

That surprised Brent, of course, and the Bobcats were now

scrambling to clog up the area in front of the net. Brent, the Baker Street Sports Clubber with the puck, was the only skater not swallowed up and covered by the defense.

So he did the only thing he could do. He kept it. He knew enough not to retreat. Brent faked a pass to Bugsy and then to me, switched the puck back and forth before him with his stick while streaking toward the net, brought the goalie out to meet him, and deftly backhanded in the first goal of the night.

We were as surprised as the Bobcats and almost didn't remember to congratulate Brent. He was skating around with his stick raised, and we just smiled at him. Even the crowd was slow in cheering. The goalie glumly dug out the offending puck and slid it back to center ice.

Perhaps if we hadn't looked so surprised, we might have had the Bobcats on the run and intimidated them. But it was obvious to them that we had one good stickhandler, a seemingly slow center (me), and luck on our side.

Our second goal, less than two minutes later, might have really done them in, except that we didn't have any reserves on the bench. We won the face-off again, and this time—in trying to prove that the first goal wasn't a fluke—we carefully played control hockey at their end, passing and passing and passing.

The Bobcats began to look worried. It was as if they were afraid they might have indeed had us underrated. Could we actually control the puck the rest of the night and win the crazy game 1-0?

Just when they started to wonder that, Cory scored on a long slapshot while their goalie was napping, and barely three minutes into the game we were leading 2-0.

We held them for the rest of the first period, and we could hear people buzzing about how impressive this new team was and how good they were at controlling the puck and playing defense.

No one mentioned how dead tired the offensive line was already. The only person on our bench was Jack Bastable.

There may have been those who thought the big guy was our coach. We, on the other hand, only wished we had a uniform that would fit him. Skating skill or not, any of us would have given anything we owned to put him on the ice and get a break.

The Bobcats kept switching lines and rushing at us with fresh players. It was all we could do to keep standing. I was short of breath, my legs ached, and I was thirsty. During the very few breaks, I grabbed a quick swig of water, but then it was back to the ice and the struggle.

Between periods, we were too tired to talk or listen. We didn't have to complain about not having any substitutes—it was too obvious, and there was little I could say in the way of strategy either. The only thing that came to me was the idea of stalling.

"You mean like we did in the basketball tournament?"

I nodded.

"Never work here. We can't control the puck long enough."

"It's worth a try, guys. We won't be trying to keep it from them. We'll just be buying ourselves some breathing time. Stay spread out and keep the puck moving, but stay stationary yourselves. It's our only chance. I don't see how we can score again, and they're on the verge."

That was sure true. We tried holding the puck for the first three minutes of the second period. It worked all right, but as soon as they intercepted one of our passes, they virtually led us down the ice and scored their first goal while we watched. After that, it was all Bobcats.

We played almost the entire rest of the second period in our own defending zone, miraculously interfering with their usually crisp passes. Jimmy played his heart out, but they scored every few minutes the rest of the way and led 4-2 going into the final period.

How we held them to just two more goals in the last period, I'll never know. I do know I have never experienced such bone weariness as when we sat before our lockers undressing.

It could have been worse was all we could think and say. In fact, we had scored twice and quickly, and that was the only thing that made us want to return for our second game the following week.

The most encouraging thing we learned between that game and the next was that the Bobcats were the favorites to win the championship. They had almost their entire team back from the previous year, when they had finished second in the league, first in the post-season playoffs, and showed well in the state tournament.

We had been talking dejectedly with some other players about having lost so soundly to the Bobcats when they assured us we had done well. "A lot of people were predicting that no one would score more than one goal against them this whole year. And you guys scored two in the first few minutes!"

We worked on our stamina every day, and we also worked on stalling better. No amount of stamina would make up for teams of twelve to fifteen players who could rotate in fresh bodies every few minutes.

We found out that those who tried to encourage us were right. The Bobcats went on to win the first half of the season, going undefeated, shutting out their next three straight opponents, and indeed, not having more than one goal scored on them in a game again.

Meanwhile, we won three of our next four games, admittedly against much weaker and younger opponents. Somehow the mix of ages on the teams wasn't what it should have been, and we found ourselves playing against much younger, much smaller teams. They had plenty of players, but few of them could pass and shoot and play defense.

We had been two and two going into the fifth game of the season when we faced the Cook County Cougars. They were a cute team of little kids who tried hard but were as inept against us as we had been against the Bobcats.

We scored on them so easily that when I realized that each

of us on the offensive line had a goal, I instructed the team to let the defensemen shoot until they each scored too. By the middle of the second period, Brent, Cory, Bugsy, Toby, and I had a goal each, and we led 5-0.

That's when I got the idea that we should let Jimmy score before any of us scored again. I thought it was a great idea. I had no idea how much trouble it would get us into.

The next time we took control of the puck, the offensive line took it across the blue line and into the attack zone. Our defensemen, Bugsy and Toby, hung back in our defending zone, confusing the Cougars.

Meanwhile, Jimmy came lumbering up the ice in full goalie gear. The crowd went crazy. First they murmured, then they yelled, then they started booing.

I was puzzled. I thought they would think it was interesting. I had seen teams use their goalies at the end of a game when they were trying anything and everything to tie. What was wrong with letting your goalie score when you were in a sure-win situation?

I soon found out.

6

A Ruckus

Jimmy seemed to hover just past the blue line in the Cougars' end zone for a few minutes while our opponents tried to intercept our passes. With Toby and Bugsy at the other end to protect our goal in case the Cougars happened to pick up a stray pass, the Cougars outnumbered us at their own end.

The booing was getting louder, and I was more puzzled. I motioned Bugsy to join us, and when he skated up the ice, the place went crazy. Now that the teams were even, we had little trouble passing the puck around enough to get Jimmy free. He took a couple of long shots with that gigantic stick of his, and though they missed, they brought the wrath of the entire crowd down upon us.

People began throwing things onto the ice, and the referee had to stop the action for a while. The ref skated up to me, puck in hand. "I can't tell you what to do. You wanna keep your goalie in the attack zone?"

I nodded, "You bet!"

He nodded and told the Cougars to get back into position. Just as play was about to resume, the Cougar coach threw a balled-up towel out onto the ice and gingerly stepped out himself. "Cougars! Off the ice! Now!"

The Cougars looked at each other and slowly glided toward him. He opened the door to their team box and let them pile in.

I was totally confused. The ref looked to me. I didn't know what to do. I realized later that he was giving me yet another chance to put Jimmy back in the goal, but I thought he was wondering if I had any idea why the Cougar coach was risking default by pulling his team from the ice in the middle of the action. I didn't, so I shrugged.

He took that to mean that I didn't care that I had offended this team and wasn't about to do anything about it, so he turned to the Cougar coach. "Earl, he wants to goalie down here, and there's nothing I can do about it."

The Cougar coach was a tall, lanky man with black, horn-rimmed glasses. "Well then, maybe I'll do something about it! Maybe I'll just pull my team from the ice and let Baker Street have their victory, how 'bout that?"

"That's your right, Earl. Just tell me what your wish is. If they don't get back on the ice soon, I have to disqualify 'em. Sorry."

"Well, at least let me talk to their captain."

The referee shrugged. "All right, Earl. But make it quick."

He did. He walked directly over to me. "You. Number four. You're in charge of this club, are you not?"

"Y-yes, sir."

"What do you think you're doing?"

"I, uh, I'm just trying to let everybody on my team score a goal, that's all. See, the offensive line each scored one, and then the defensemen scored—"

"I know that. So you think it would be real cute to show us up, to make us look bad, to humiliate my little team that hasn't won a game all season by letting your goalie come down here and score too?"

"It's not that! I didn't realize that it would look like that at all. I just—"

"Well, I'm not gonna let you do it. I'm not going to subject these young athletes to this kind of unsportsmanlike conduct. This is one good reason why they shouldn't allow teams to be in this league without adult supervision."

I was stunned.

He turned to the referee. "That's it, John. Call the game. I'm pullin' my team out."

I could hardly believe it. And I couldn't let it happen. "No! Wait! I didn't realize! I didn't mean to make anyone look bad. I'll put my goalie back in the goal, and we'll take it easy on your kids from here on out. But don't quit, OK?"

The ref looked at the coach. "It sounds reasonable, Earl. That's all I can say. Now you've got about ten seconds to make up your mind. We've got two more games to get in here tonight. What'll it be?"

"All right, we'll play, but give me a few more seconds with the Baker Street captain here." He waved his players back onto the ice, and Jimmy, who had heard the conversation, hustled back to the net at our end.

The coach moved closer to me, looking strange trying to keep his balance on the ice in his street shoes. "Listen, I appreciate that you're young and maybe you didn't realize what you were doin'. Did you hear that crowd? They thought it was bush league right off the bat."

He was pointing in my face now, and it was all I could do to keep from bursting into tears. "But let me tell you this, son. You put your goalie back, and you insist you didn't do this on purpose, and I'll accept that. But don't you dare take it easy on my team the rest of the way. That's more insulting than showing us up by having your goalie come down here and try to score on us. Understand?"

I didn't, but I knew I would when I had a calm moment to think about it. I nodded. "Don't take it easy on you, even though we're up five to zip and will probably score some more?"

"You've got it!"

I nodded again and play resumed. At the end of two

45

periods we led 7-1, and the referee skated over to me. "Look, if you want your goalie to score too, which would be a record in this league—everybody scorin' at least once in the same game—you ought to just put somebody else in the goal, with the equipment on. Put your goalie on the offensive line, and let him take his shots."

I was doubtful. "Wouldn't that upset the other coach?"

"Nah. That kind of switching goes on around here all the time. Just don't send your fully equipped goalie into the attack zone, that's all."

We had just enough time to put Cory in the goal with the oversized equipment on. The other coach said nothing. The fans didn't boo. And with three minutes left in the game, Jimmy put us up 9 to 1 with his first and what would prove to be his only goal of the season. The look on his face made it worth it.

When the Cougars scored twice in the closing minutes, I was afraid I was going to have some explaining to do to their coach. I was prepared to tell him that we had no substitutes, that we were dead tired, that our new goalie was small and inexperienced, and that his team really wasn't all that bad.

But he didn't give me the chance. I stared at him when they scored, and he was cheering like the rest of the team. I knew if he thought we had handed them those goals, he would have glared at me, so I guessed he was giving Baker Street the benefit of the doubt.

A few weeks later, when we faced the Cougars again for the first game of the second half, their coach was friendly before the game. "I want you to know that I believe you didn't mean to show us up in that first game."

I smiled. "I'm glad, because you're right."

"That's what your friends tell me."

"My team said that?"

"No, the friends you have gained in this league on the other teams. They're pretty impressed with you and your players."

"That's nice to hear."

"Oh, they told me all about you and your baseball and basketball and football teams."

"Yeah, we play soccer too."

"Do you?"

I nodded, embarrassed.

"Well, good for you, Dallas. I like that. I'm proud of you and hope you do well. Finishing fourth in the first half during your first season in this league is nothing to sneeze at. You know if you do that well in the second half, you make the playoffs. Personally, I hope you make it and win it."

"Do you really think we could?"

He chuckled. "No, I guess not. Not really. But it sure would be nice to see. You see, the thing that riled me so much when I thought you were trying to rub that loss in our faces is that that's the type of thing I've faced in this league for the last several years. I try to follow the rules and regulations to the best of my abilities, and it hurts to lose out to teams that I know are cheating."

Cheating? Was that what he thought? I couldn't let that pass. "We certainly didn't intend to cheat, and in fact, even though I see now why what we did was offensive to you, it wasn't cheating."

"Oh, I know that. But I'm talking about teams that really do cheat. Falsifying birth certificates. Using kids who don't really live in the area. That type of a thing. You know, I think you're the only team in the top four that I wouldn't accuse of having several illegal players."

I was glad he and I had had a good talk and that he thought better of us, but I was shocked by what he had said. Was it possible? That much cheating going on? I would have been disappointed to discover *any* cheating, let alone on at least three teams.

Did the league wink at such a breaking of the rules? I wondered why the Cougar coach didn't take his accusations to the league president. The champions of our league represented our part of the state in the state tournament. How

47

would it look if our champs did well and then it was discovered that they had cheated?

I thought about what the Cougar couch had said during the whole game against them that night. I didn't play well, didn't score, didn't even get an assist. We won 5-1, but it was obvious to my teammates that I was not myself. Toby brought it up in the locker room.

"We're doing pretty well, Dal. How come you're so out of it? We start the second half off with a good victory, tryin' to finish at least fourth again and get into the playoffs, and you're playin' like you left your head somewhere."

I apologized and told the guys the whole story on the way home. When we arrived at my place and the others were calling their parents for rides home, Brent asked if he could talk to me. That was something new. The little blond, one of the fastest runners and skaters I'd ever seen, was generally pretty quiet.

If he wanted to talk, I wanted to listen.

7

Brent's Bombshell

Brent shocked me. "Dallas, I think I'd better drop out of the Baker Street Sports Club. One of the other guys will fit into my hockey uniform."

I didn't know what to say. What would we do without Brent? He was a great kid and a great athlete. He had been good in every sport for us with his small size and his super speed. "What's the problem, Brent? I didn't know anything was wrong."

"I'm not sure anything is wrong, Dallas. I just feel like I don't belong anymore."

"How can you say that? You haven't missed a meeting or a practice since we started the club. You're a charter member, you've never been in trouble, never broken a rule. Who's made you feel unwelcome?"

He fidgeted and then looked at me, his longish blond hair flapping in the breeze over his forehead. "You have."

"*I* have? Me?"

"You, Dallas."

I wanted to know more, to ask him to be more specific, but I was speechless. I had always tried to make everyone feel like a part of the club, but there were some guys you didn't feel you had to worry about. Brent was one of those. "What have I done? Whatever it was I didn't mean it."

Brent looked as if the conversation was as painful for him as it was for me. "I'm not part of the crowd."

"The crowd? We don't have a crowd, Brent. What have you been left out of?"

"It just seems like you spend more time with Jimmy and Cory."

I couldn't argue with that. "Jimmy has always been my friend, since long before we even started the Baker Street Sports Club. In fact, since we moved out here years ago, he's been my friend. And Cory goes to my church."

"So you are with them everyday?"

"Not everyday."

"Almost."

"OK, almost. We have a little Bible study that we do together. Is that what you're talking about?"

Brent nodded.

"Well, Brent, you're certainly welcome to join us. I had no idea you might want to be involved in that."

"You never asked."

"No, I never did. I guess I just thought that, uh, that—"

"That since I don't go to church that I wouldn't be interested."

"Well, yeah, sort of. I mean, it's not like I haven't asked you to go to church, you know."

"I know. My parents won't let me go to church. They've got something against some church or some pastor or something, and they don't want me getting involved. But I could join you guys for whatever it is you're doing, and it wouldn't be like I was going to church and disobeying my parents."

I was curious. "Do you want to be involved with us on this just because you think we're the special crowd of the club?"

Brent shook his head. "I was really just saying that to get your attention, so maybe you'd feel bad about leaving me out."

"Well, it worked."

He smiled. "I haven't been to church or Sunday school or even that summer time thing they have—"

"Vacation Bible school."

"Yeah, for about five years. I liked it. I learned a lot. I thought it was fun. Now I can hardly remember what it was all about."

"Well, do you know when and where we meet and what we do?"

"'Course! Everyone knows! Jimmy and Cory brag about it all the time!"

Oh, so that was it! Something that Jimmy and Cory and I were doing on our own, as friends and Christians, was causing a problem within the club. "Are the other guys upset about it too?"

"I don't know. It's hard to tell. Both Bugsy and Toby say they're glad they haven't been asked because they don't want to come. They don't want to get religious."

"We're not religious!"

"Well, what do you call it?"

"It's not a religion. It's a person. It's Jesus."

"I know that. And you're saying that's not religion?"

I shook my head. "That's what I'm saying."

"But it makes you guys nicer, and you don't get all mad about things. If it's not religion, how come my parents are so angry about it?"

"Maybe what they're angry about is a religious problem. Our little Bible study and our church aren't about religion. They're about Jesus."

"That's what I want to learn about. Will I have to pray?"

"You don't want to pray?"

"Not out loud in front of people."

"Then you don't have to."

"Do I have to get saved?"

"Do you know what that means?"

"Not really. I think you join something and get baptized

and say something in front of people, right?"

I shook my head.

"See, Dallas, there's a lot I need to learn."

"I know. And to answer your question, no, you don't have to do anything to study with us. We just tell each other what we want to pray about, and then we pray for each other. You wouldn't have to do that if you didn't want to, but you could still tell us what you wanted us to pray about. Like we could pray that your mom and dad would think again about letting you go to church."

He nodded.

"And then we read a story out of a devotional book, read something from the Old and New Testaments of the Bible, and memorize a verse a week."

"A verse from the Bible?"

"Right."

"That's what we used to do at that summer vacation thing."

"Vacation Bible school."

"Uh-huh."

"So you still want to do it?"

"Yes!"

"See you tomorrow right after school, right here."

He didn't stay around long enough to agree. His mother had pulled up in the driveway. She looked pleasant enough and waved at me from the car.

Jimmy and Cory weren't sure what they thought about the idea that Brent would be joining us. "He's not even a Christian, is he?"

"No, but he doesn't know it. He's confused about where Jesus fits in with church and religion and our daily meetings. He was worried about whether he had to be saved, but he didn't even remember from Vacation Bible school what that was all about."

"Then how is he supposed to get anything out of our Bible study? He doesn't want to pray with us, and he's not a Christian."

I shook my head and found myself growing sarcastic. "Oh, OK, let's not let him into our little clique. I mean, he doesn't qualify, and we wouldn't want him messing up anything. Besides, he might learn what it's all about, and surely there are enough Christians around. We don't need any more, do we?"

Jimmy and Cory looked at me strangely. Jimmy smiled. "OK, O'Neil, we get the point. Back off a little, huh?"

"Well, have either of you ever told anyone else about Jesus?"

They both nodded. "You know we have. Lots of people at school and even the guys in the club."

"But you wouldn't want one of 'em joining us when we study and learn more?"

"We already got that point, OK, Dallas?"

"OK, I'm just saying that if we let Brent in, one of us might get to help him become a Christian. Wouldn't that be great?"

We talked quite a bit longer before our meeting the next day, because I wanted to make sure Cory and Jimmy knew that we shouldn't put a lot of pressure on Brent at first.

"Let's just include him. Let him listen and read and share prayer requests, whatever he wants. He can discuss, ask questions, whatever. But don't make him feel like an outsider, and let's not make him feel second class because he hasn't received Christ yet."

As it turned out, Brent was the one who made us feel bad. He was a quick learner, very eager to get involved. He liked to read aloud, and even though he didn't pray with us, he said he would pray about our requests when he was home alone.

He read the Bible and the lesson book, and he asked a lot of good questions. He seemed to have the freshness about it all that we had lost. After several weeks, he started asking really hard questions. That's when we started feeling the pressure.

For instance, he wanted to know why, if we really believed that people who didn't become true, born again Christians would go to hell when they died, we didn't tell everyone we knew. "Are you afraid they'll think you're crazy?"

We admitted that was true. I tried to explain. "It takes a lot of boldness. People don't believe it right away, for one thing."

"But God will give you the courage and the words, right?"

We nodded.

"And do you believe that if I don't pray and receive Christ, I'll go to hell?"

We looked at each other. I spoke. "What do you think, Brent?"

"Seems pretty clear to me. Were you guys gonna tell me this, or not?"

"Eventually. It sounds like you picked it up without our needing to come right out with it."

"But what if I hadn't? And what if I had been hit by a car or struck by lightning or something?"

We looked down, none of us knowing what to say.

Jimmy spoke up. "So now that you know, what are you going to do about it?"

Brent smiled. "Just give you guys a hard time. There's a lot more we have to do with all we know from our studying. Like we have to tell the league about the teams that are cheating. That's something we can't let just pass by. We can't pretend we don't see when bad things happen. They have to be made right."

I knew he was right, but I was still curious. "Brent, Jimmy asked you a serious question. We didn't want to push you, didn't want to offend you, didn't want to turn you away. But now it's clear that you know what this is all about. What're you going to do?"

"Nothing."

"Nothing?"

He smiled. "I already did it. Last night. And now I'm telling you, which is the next step. And if it's all right, I'd like you to help me talk my parents into letting me come to church with you."

"Sure!"

"It won't be easy, you know. They're not going to be happy about all of this."

"You haven't told them what you've done?"

He shook his head.

"You're going to leave that to us?"

He shrugged. "I don't know. All I know is that I feel like I should be going to church, and I don't have any more courage about asking my parents if I can than you guys do to tell your best friends about Jesus."

8

Stirring Up Trouble

The regular league season was winding down. The Baker Street Sports Club had done fairly well in the second half, though our last game was against the fourth place team, the McLain County Mustangs. We were in fifth by a half game, so a victory would give us fourth and an automatic berth in the post-season playoffs. A tie or a loss would leave the Mustangs in fourth, and we'd have to play them again to see who made the playoffs.

We wanted to win badly, and we wanted to win now. We had got in much better shape, and a couple of our guys were among the leaders in the league in scoring. Brent was fourth in goals, and I was sixth in assists. Jimmy had one of the lowest goals-scored-against statistics, which was remarkable for the goalie of a fourth and fifth place team. What it showed was that though we lost our share of games, we generally kept them close.

I knew that if we had had the money for more equipment, we could have fared much better in the league, because we had learned puck control and good defense. If we had the stamina for a better, more sustained and consistent offense, we would have been in good shape. The talent was there. The bench strength was not.

I told the club that Brent had raised the issue of the teams who apparently cheated by having out-of-the-area players or who had falsified birth certificates. "He thinks we should tell the league and encourage some action against them."

Toby said he agreed. "But will the league do anything about it? The league officials must already know and figure it's OK."

I admitted I didn't know. "Regardless, we have to decide whether to stir it up. It's not fair. It doesn't fit in with our own club's rules and regulations. And it's not the type of league we want to see for kids."

Jimmy suggested that we threaten to drop out. "We'd sorta have to if they ignored the problem, wouldn't we?"

We all agreed on that.

Bugsy asked if we knew who the offending teams and players were. "Or will you have to talk to that Earl guy again, the coach of the Cook County Cougars?"

I said I probably would have to. "Anybody know his last name?"

No one responded. Toby spoke up again. "Why doesn't *he* complain?"

I cocked my head. "Doesn't seem to have the backbone for it."

"When he thought we were showing him up, he didn't hesitate to tell you off, Dallas."

"Yeah. I guess hasslin' a twelve-year-old is a whole different thing than getting some of your fellow coaches in trouble."

"Right! That's one advantage you've got. You're not really a coach like them. You're a player, a team captain. They can't get too upset with you."

"Wanna bet? Wait till we raise this issue."

That night as we prepared to take on the McLain County Mustangs, I sought out the referee, John Lucas. "Mr. Lucas, do you know the last name of the coach of the Cougars?"

"Conlan. They play tonight too, ya know."

"Do they? After us?"

He nodded. "He should be around. You wanna talk to him if I see him?"

"Yes, thanks."

"You guys aren't still mad at each other, are you?"

"Nah! We got all that straightened out a long time ago."

"That's good. He had a point, you know. You guys *were* showing them up, even though I knew you didn't mean to."

"You *knew* that?"

"Well, not at first. In fact, when I kept trying to give you a chance to change it before the crowd and the other team and their coach got ugly, I thought you were really doing it with a vengeance. But then I saw that it was just that you didn't realize. Hey, there's Conlan now. Earl! Earl! You got a minute?"

He waved Earl Conlan over and left us alone.

I wasn't sure where to begin. "Uh, yeah, I've been meanin' to talk to you about something you said a few weeks ago."

"You mean that flap about you guys tryin' to show us up? Don't give it another thought. I chalked it off to immaturity. Forget it."

"No, it wasn't that. It was what you said about other teams cheating."

He stared at me.

"I was just wonderin' why you never said anything to the league about it and how you would feel if I did."

He said nothing, just looked at me over the top of his horn-rims.

I got the feeling I had hit on a sore spot. "Shouldn't something be done about it? You said we were the only team in the top four that you wouldn't accuse of having several illegal players. Not one, you said, but several. Did you mean that?"

He nodded, still not speaking.

61

"Yet you don't feel it's serious enough to go to the league with it?"

He scratched his cheek. "It's serious enough, kid. It's just that no one listens to the coach of a last place team. And when you've got three or four teams all flauntin' the rules, they have to have some connections to the board, if you know what I mean."

"No, I don't know what you mean. Tell me."

"Just that with that many teams involved, surely there's a parent or a former coach or even a former player who knows about this and who serves on the board and doesn't do anything about it."

"Do you think the whole board knows?"

"I'd like to hope not."

"The president?"

"I don't know. I sincerely hope not."

"How would you feel about my finding out, Mr. Conlan?"

He took to staring at me again. This was one scared man. "You wouldn't be using my name now, would you, O'Neil?"

"You mean *you* have players that are—"

"No! I just mean that you're not going to say you got this idea from me, are you?"

"Does that mean you're not going to stand behind me if I take this to the board?"

"You got that right! I'm out of it, you understand?"

"But I need information. I can't go to the board without some idea of which teams are cheating and which kids are ineligible. They'll laugh me out of the place."

"There's also another problem you're gonna face, Dallas. They're gonna think you're just tryin' to improve your showing in the playoffs. If you can get a team in trouble, get it to default on a bunch of its games—forfeit 'em, you know—why, then it brings you up a notch in the standings. See?"

"That's not why I would do it!"

"Maybe not, but that's what it's gonna look like. Why don't you do like I do and leave it alone? You and your friends had fun here, didn't you? You're gonna probably win tonight and get yourself into the playoffs where you'll do OK but lose to a team with a couple of thirteen- maybe fourteen-year-olds on it, maybe a couple from outside their county, and that'll be the end of that. The board looks the other way, you look the other way, nobody's really hurt. Huh?"

I studied him. "I can tell you don't like it any more than I do, Mr. Conlan. There must be a reason why it gripes you enough to tell me about it and yet it scares you enough to stay away from it and encourage me to do the same."

He was staring again, but a look came over his face as if he had just thought of something or just discovered something. "I'll make you a deal. If you are bound and determined to take this to the board, I'll tell you whatever you need to know. I'll give you team names, coaches' names, and ineligible players' names. But you never say where you got your information, even if they ask you point blank if you got it from me."

"I can't lie."

"You don't have to. You just tell 'em right off the bat that you won't say where you got any of your information and that if they suggest a name, you won't comment. Fair enough?"

I shrugged. "It sounds fair, but you really changed the subject on me. I had asked you why you're so afraid of this."

"Your answer will come with the information, son, but we can't be seen together anymore. People might remember seeing us talking after you blow the lid off this. Let's decide on a place to meet. I'll give you whatever you need."

"I don't know. You want to come to my house after your game tonight?"

"Sure. As long as I know no one would be following me. You sure it's all right with your folks?"

"I'll clear it as soon as I get home."

63

9

A Meeting with the Board

Several hours later, after the Baker Street Sports Club had eked out a 6-5 victory and assured itself of a spot in the post-season playoffs, Earl Conlan sat across from me at our dining room table. My parents were in the living room, reading.

I had filled them in on everything that was going on, and as usual my dad said he trusted me to do the right thing and to let him know if I needed any help. "No matter what happens, Dal, I hope you're prepared for the fact that you're going to make yourself some enemies."

Mr. Conlan said he had thought a lot about what he might tell me. "And I decided to make it easy for you. I have written here the names of four teams and their coaches and listed the players that I either know or suspect are not eligible. Some of this is based on hearsay from my own players, but most of it is based on personal knowledge, my being told firsthand by one of these coaches."

"He was trying to get you to do the same?"

"Very vigorously."

"And you refused?"

"Yes, but not as vehemently as I should have."

"Why not?"

"You'll see. Just read the lists. You may copy them if you wish, but I want my original back so I can destroy it. I don't even want to risk someone recognizing my handwriting.'"

I began to wonder if I wanted to be involved in this if the stakes were so high. Did he actually fear for his life? I asked him.

"Oh, no. Nothing like that. Just future relationships. You'll see."

I could wait no longer. I opened the neatly penned sheet before me and read the names. Leon Poors coached the first place Bay City Bobcats. Three players were listed as suspect. Morgan Gilbert coached the second place Lake County Lions. Two of their players were doubtful. Wes Conlan coached the third place DeKalb County Tigers. Three players were listed. Dallas O'Neil captained the Baker Street Sports Club. Jack Bastable was listed as ineligible.

"He doesn't even play!"

Mr. Conlan smiled at me. "I know that. I put down what I'd heard. I've seen the boy. He must be six foot seven and in college, right? Rumors are that you plan to suit him up one of these times and claim he's twelve."

"The fact is, he's six-four, can't skate, is retarded, and *is* twelve."

"I don't believe it."

"In the case of the Baker Street Sports Club, we have the papers to prove it."

"I'm sure you do. Read on."

I read that Hamilton Harding was coach of the McLain Country Mustangs and that one of his players was listed. I looked up.

Earl Conlan looked at me pensively. "You missed it."

"Missed what?"

He motioned to the paper. I looked again. That time it jumped out at me. Wes *Conlan*, coach of the Tigers. "Related to you?"

"Oh, yes."

"Brother?"

He nodded. "Younger brother."

"Really?"

He nodded again. "Always better than I in every sport. Couldn't beat him in anything. Nothing. A foot race. Throwing a ball for distance. Scoring in youth league hockey. Tennis. Card games. Table games, for cryin' out loud. I almost didn't coach in this league because I knew he would be better than I would be year after year. And he has been. But he said they desperately needed someone and that the league wasn't competitive."

"Not competitive? I've found it *very* competitive. What did he mean by that?"

"He meant that it was for the purpose of instruction, training. That everyone got a chance to play and that it was for the kids, not for the adults. He didn't admit that he would, of course, still coach better than I and have better records, but he insisted that that shouldn't make any difference since it was all for fun."

"And you didn't find it that way?"

"You tell me. You captain a team in this league. We play for blood, do we not?"

"Seems we do. Our club likes it."

"Do you like playing against cheaters?"

"Some of the teams on this list have been pretty hard to beat."

"Impossible, to look at your record. The Mustangs are the only team you beat, and they have only one illegal player."

I sat thinking. "I'm taking this to the league, Mr. Conlan."

"And you'll leave me out of it?"

"If I must."

"You must. My little brother already thinks I'm crazy to play by the rules, but he'd never forgive me if I turned on him and turned him in. Who knows what the rest of the family would think of me?"

"And that's what's most important to you?"

"Isn't it to you?"

I had to think about that. "No. I can't imagine my family ever holding it against me if I was doing what I thought was right."

"Well, you're young yet. You'll learn what's most important. You'll find that justice can take a back seat to diplomacy at times."

I hoped that day would never come. I copied Mr. Conlan's notes, watched him tear his original into little pieces before throwing it into our fireplace, then shook hands with him. It took me a long time to get to sleep that night, thinking what a sad, weak man he was.

It wasn't easy to get a meeting before the entire league board. I nearly had to let on what I wanted to talk about just to get them to call a special meeting. All I said was that I had things to talk about that affected the future of the league and even impacted the playoffs, which were about to begin.

Jimmy and Cory said they would be praying for me during the time of the closed session with the league board. Brent said his father told him that if I could get any action out of that board, he'd let Brent go to church with me. He thought our cause was a just and good one, and his promise made me want to succeed more than ever.

I began respectfully and carefully, thanking the board for allowing me the time. "And now, let me get straight to my point. I would like the league to look into the exact legal ages and addresses of the following players from the following teams."

I read them off to a stunned, stony silence. A few of the men were smoking. No one moved.

Finally, the league president, Mr. Howard Robinson, spoke. He sounded as if he was unimpressed. "Uh, Mr. O'Neil. Could you tell this board why we should check into all these players? They were screened at the time of their registrations."

"I have reason to believe that every one of them is ineligible, either because of being too old or not living within the area covered by the rules."

"Says who?"

"I will not be saying where I got my information except that it is from reliable sources."

"We can't track down every rumor that crops up, young man. Especially now when the tournament is about to begin."

I started to speak, but another board member interrupted. "What are you asking us to do, O'Neil?"

"Just to check them out. That shouldn't take too long. Look at birth certificates, letters from parents about where they live, ask a few questions. That's all."

"Sounds reasonable."

"No, it doesn't! It sounds like a wild goose chase intended to delay the tournament or benefit this team that just barely qualified."

I had to speak to that. "I thought that possibility might be brought up. Let me say that the Baker Street Sports Club is willing to drop out and consider itself ineligible for the playoffs during any investigation if that is the wish of this board."

"Why are you doing this, son?"

"I just want to see the league have a high standard for fairness. I assumed you would all want that too."

"We do. We just don't know why we should suspect a list of players on your say so."

"You don't have to. But I believe you'll find cheating and that you'll want to do something about it."

"Would you care to put your request in the form of an official protest of the outcome of one of your games? For instance, I know you lost to the Bobcats four times this year. If you believe one of their players—and you say there are three—is ineligible, protest the game, and we can officially check it out."

"OK, if that's how it is supposed to go."

"You're aware that each file of a protest requires a fifty dollar deposit?"

"No, sir, and our club is broke. It took every penny we had to get equipment and register for this league. We have six players on our entire team. We would not be able to pay for a protest, even if we knew we were going to get the money back. We've spent hundreds and hundreds of dollars to play in this league, and we expected it to be fair."

An older gentleman spoke. "And well you should have. I expect that if we don't investigate this, you'll run to the newspapers, the same ones who write up your club all the time, and tell them the whole story."

"I hadn't thought of that, sir. But it's not a bad idea." That brought a burst of laughter from some, scowls from others. "Seriously, I know I wouldn't have to consider that because I'm sure you'll at least want to check out a few of these. You want a fair league as much as we do."

Mr. Robinson stood. "Dallas, we appreciate your bringing this before us. We'll consider it in private, and we'll let you know what we decide. Fair enough?"

I'd heard the same question from Earl Conlan. And I responded to Mr. Robinson the same way I had to Mr. Conlan. For the next several days, I waited for his call.

But when it came, it was not at all what I expected.

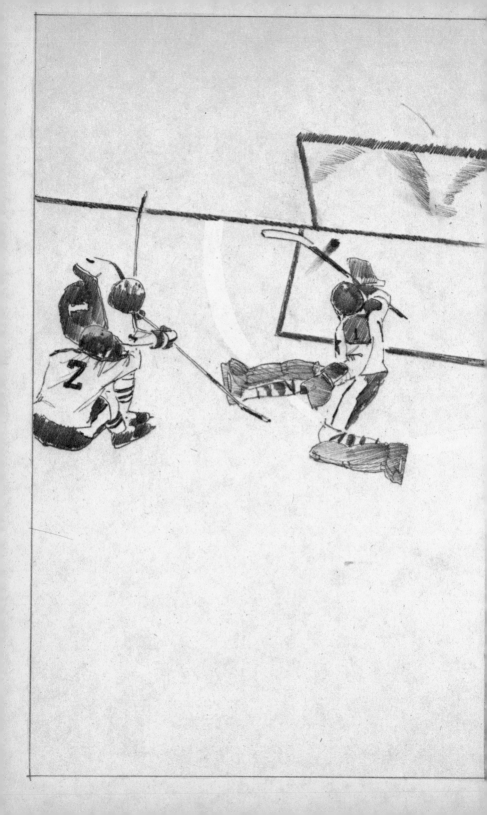

10

The Decision

My mother told me that I was to call a Mr. Robinson. My hands shook as I punched his number. I figured he would be telling me that they had either decided to investigate my charges or not, but he surprised me. "We would like to meet with you privately one more time, at your convenience."

"Tomorrow night?"

"If that's all right with you." He was being so formal I hardly knew how to react.

The next night I was ushered in before the board again. From the looks on their faces, I would have guessed that they had decided to turn down my request, and I was frankly impressed that they had the courage and decency to tell me themselves. The only other possibility that crossed my mind was that they had discovered who had given me my information and that they were going to make him out as some sort of criminal or at least a liar.

I was wrong on both counts. Mr. Robinson spoke. "Dallas, we not only decided to do as you ask, but we have already done it. We began by checking just one name from each of the teams you listed, and in the end we checked not only all you gave us, but also every registered player in our league. We want to thank you for bringing this to our attention, and before we announce our findings and our rulings to the entire league, we wanted to tell you personally.

"First of all, every player on every team you named was found ineligible. There were also a couple more from each of the top three teams. In our investigation, we also found that you had preliminarily registered a Jack Bastable, who has never suited up but who caused quite a bit of consternation among the other coaches, both offending and innocent ones."

"But he's—"

"Please let me finish, Mr. O'Neil. I will give you a chance to speak if you still care to when I am done. We want you to know that Jack Bastable's age and residence have been cleared by our subcommittee of regulations. If you care to suit him up in the future, he is registered and eligible.

"As for the offending teams, each will forfeit every game it played in which the ineligible players participated. It should not surprise you that in every case, except for the team that had only one ineligible player, that will cost the top three teams every game they won this season."

"You mean, I mean, the playoffs and—?"

Mr. Robinson held up a hand. "That means what it means. The top three teams wind up with no victories and no ties. The fifth place team winds up with, I believe, two victories." He glanced at an associate who nodded that he was correct.

"We have decided, Dallas, to not terminate any of the coaches who have offended in this way. You may not understand that, and I must say that it was a matter of much discussion on this board. Many of us would have preferred that course, were it not advised against by our legal counsel."

"I don't understand."

"It simply means that we do not want to face the lawsuits that might arise from our implying that a man had flagrantly flaunted the rules of our league. We can and will and have, however, forced forfeits of all those games we mentioned, and

74

that will undoubtedly result in the resignation of each coach."

"What are you going to do about the playoffs?"

"Nothing will change, Dallas. The top four teams will compete in the playoffs."

"But you said the top three forfeited—"

"By forfeiting their games, the top three teams are now in a dead heat for sixth place with no victories. They will not be in the playoffs. Your team wins the regular season championship and becomes the favorite, number one seed in the playoffs."

"And if we win we go to the state tournament?"

"That's how it works."

"But we'll get destroyed."

"That's likely. But the credibility of our league will remain intact. And we'll be proud to have you represent us. Let's not get ahead of ourselves though, son. Don't forget that this will give new life and hope to the other second division teams, who have mostly never made the playoffs before."

Was he ever right about that! You can guess who our toughest competition was. None other than the Cook County Cougars. The league was wild with stories and rumors and noisiness about the scandal, but the beautiful thing about it was that even my name was kept out of it.

The league board made it appear that they had done the investigation on their own. They refused to tell who came forward with information. Mr. Conlan's brother accused him, of course, but I doubt he admitted anything. I know he didn't let on that it was I who had gone forward.

The playoffs were tough. We finally beat the Cougars by 1 in overtime to qualify for the state tournament, one in which we knew we didn't belong. After the game, Earl Conlan shook my hand, as is customary, but he pumped it vigorously and looked into my eyes, his own filling with tears.

I still felt sorry for him and wished he were braver, but I was happy for him. He felt better. Justice had been done and, in a way, he had been responsible.

At the state tournament, I did a lot of scouting. There was a clear favorite and a more than clear underdog (guess who?). The favorites were the Green Valley Braves, who had won the tournament the last three years in a row, and in their local league they had finished with three shutouts, not to mention going undefeated the whole year.

They were most impressive in practice, looking confident, almost smug. They all wore little pins, souvenirs from previous state tournaments, which were designed to make most of the rest of us feel like the newcomers we really were.

I was shocked to see them lose the first night. The tournament was a double elimination affair where the first four teams who lost went immediately into a losers' bracket and could still win the state championship if they didn't lose again. Lose twice, and you're out.

The Carbondale Cardinals played a rough-and-tumble defensive game and led 2-0 until the last minute when the Braves mounted a furious attack, scored once, and then had three straight super shots turned away as the horn sounded. The Braves were good sports about it, but it was obvious they had been soundly surprised.

In the other first-round game that night, the Peoria Bombers whipped the Rockford Raiders 8-1 in a game that was actually more impressive even than the lopsided score indicates. I didn't hope that Baker Street would get the chance to play the Bombers, a team decked out in light- and dark-blue uniforms with a big five-pointed star on their chests. Still I was most taken with the man who would be defending me if we did.

He was number 18, a husky kid who looked about twice my size. His bulk didn't slow him down. He was a fast, powerful skater, a good stickhandler, a violent but fair body checker, and seemingly impossible to get around.

The next night the Normal Knights edged the Pontiac Panthers, and then it was our turn to take to the ice. We faced the East St. Louis Eagles, who were no strangers to state competition either. This was their fourth state tourney in a row, and they had finished first four years before.

Maybe they were overconfident. Maybe we were psyched up. Maybe we had finally got in shape and peaked. Whatever the reason, we found ourselves able to play even with them the whole way. It was remarkable, especially to us. With five minutes to go in the third period, we actually led 4-3, but we were fading fast.

They were beating us to every puck, and we were staggering, huffing and puffing. They were deep with fresh bodies, and we were holding on for dear life. I firmly believe that if they had just played smart, patient hockey, they could have at least tied us and probably overtaken us.

But as the minutes ebbed away from them, they panicked. They pulled their goalie from the net and put another man on the ice. They nearly scored, but Jimmy made two miraculous saves. The second one bounced high in the air right in front of him, and for some reason I headed up the ice toward the blue line. He saw me, and as the puck came down, he batted at it like a baseball player.

It bounced twice and hit my stick, then slid past me into the attack zone. I gave chase but couldn't catch it. I didn't need to. Jimmy had picked up an assist, and I had scored a goal! The Eagles were broken. They played frantic hockey now, making mistake after mistake and allowing us yet another goal.

We could hardly believe it, but we were in the winners bracket, at least after the first round. We would play the Carbondale Cards, the Peoria Bombers would play the Pontiac Panthers, and, in the losers bracket, the Green Valley Braves would play East St. Louis, and Rockford would play Normal.

The double losers would be out, the losers from the winners bracket would play the winners from the losers bracket, and if that wasn't confusing enough, we actually started thinking about surprising everyone and winning the crazy tournament.

It was silly, but you have to have a dream.

11

The Big Finish

No one could believe it when the defending state champion Green Valley Braves lost to the team that we had beaten in the first round, the East St. Louis Eagles. Actually, everyone thought that the Braves would breeze through the losers bracket and come back to win the championship the way they had the year before.

But the Braves looked listless, and rumors began to fly. Had they lost on purpose for some reason? What reason? Was there another suspicious team in the tournament? Sure there was. The Baker Street Sports Club. Here we were, a team that had virtually backed into the tournament, and we had won. People started checking into us, asking a lot of questions, but of course not asking us.

In the other bracket, Pontiac surprised the Peoria Bombers in a high-scoring donnybrook, 10-8. There had been several fights in that game. No one doubted that Peoria would come back to battle for the finals in that bracket, but then, after the Green Valley surprise, who knew what would happen?

By the time we were set to take the ice against heavily favored Carbondale, the suspicious minds had found the right—or wrong—source of information about us. Mr. Con-

Ian's brother had finally figured the whole thing out or had been tipped off by a sympathetic board member, and he was telling anyone who'd listen that I was an unscrupulous person.

It was all over the ice arena that we had cheated our way into our own league playoffs and that we had no business in the state tournament. The newspapers, who had written us up as the Cinderella team in the tournament because we were new and had a mediocre league record, now came asking questions about the scandal.

Brent, who had delivered the good news that his father was going to allow him to come to church with me, was puzzled by this new development. "This is what you get when you do the right thing?"

I nodded. "You bet. Look what happened to Jesus, and He never did *anything* wrong."

Regardless, none of us could concentrate on the game. We looked like the pretenders we were and were whipped 5-0 by the Cardinals. They would move on to play the winner of the other bracket, the Pontiac Panthers, while we played the East St. Louis Eagles again for the right to play the winner of the other losers bracket, either Rockford or Peoria. We were hoping it would be Rockford, of course, after seeing them lose big, but it was Peoria who had beat them, so there was little chance of that.

Truthfully, I thought East St. Louis would mutilate us this time around. They should have seen that they simply quit too early the last time, but we could see by the looks in their eyes at the start of the game that they figured they had lost to us once, they would lose to us again. We obliged them.

It went pretty much like the first game against them, except that we built a bigger lead earlier, and they bailed out long before it was over. Now the Cards and Baker Street were the only teams in the top bracket who hadn't been eliminated by a second loss.

Peoria made mincemeat of Rockford in the other losers

bracket, beating them 11-2, and the Raiders wouldn't have scored at all had not the Bombers put in their reserves for the entire last period.

The Cards beat Pontiac in a close 4-3 game to remain the only undefeated team. That allowed them to sit and wait for the rest of us to eliminate each other until only one other team would be left with one loss. That team would play the Cardinals, and if they won they would play them again for the championship. If they lost, of course, they would have two losses, and the Cards would be unbeaten champs.

Pontiac, having made it to the last game in the winners bracket before losing, would play the winner of our game against Peoria for the right to face the Cards again. Suddenly we realized that even if we lost, we would not finish lower than fourth in the state, and we had finished fourth in our league before all the forfeits!

I began getting hate letters delivered to the locker room, accusing me of cheating, of paying teams to lose, and all kinds of other wild things. I tried to keep it from the other players, but that was impossible.

·It made it very difficult to concentrate on our game against one of the most powerful young hockey teams we had ever seen, the Peoria Bombers. Watching them warm up, it was difficult to imagine that they had lost to anyone. Apparently, they had let down on defense while scoring all those points, because defense had been their strongest asset before that.

I called the team together. "We all know we shouldn't be here. We also all know that we are not guilty of all the things everyone is accusing us of. This could be our last game of the season, but even if it is, I want to go down fighting. This team's only loss was a high scoring game that embarrassed them because of their reputation for defense. That tells me that they are going to do everything in their power to shut us out."

Bugsy was gazing out across the ice at their size and strength and speed. "They could do it."

"I know they could, but let's play some defense ourselves. While they're concentrating on shutting us out, let's see if we can keep their scoring machine shut off as much as possible. If we don't, the game will get away from us real quick."

I was quickly losing the guys' attention. They kept sneaking peeks at the Bombers. They were something.

Toby turned back. "Hey! Let's not let them beat us before the game starts, huh?"

It was good advice. We knelt together with our hands clasped and shouted encouragement to one another. The game began.

The Bombers were more than we expected. They won the face off and attacked our zone. They passed and shot and passed and shot and checked and banged us off the boards. They were all over us. Somehow, I can't even say how, we kept stifling their shots.

Jimmy saved several, but Toby and Bugsy were playing over their heads too. They kept diving, juking, poking, and frustrating the big Bombers. For more than six minutes, the puck stayed at our end of the ice while we frantically tried to smother it.

When we finally cleared the puck away, I just skated it to center ice and stood there protecting it with my stick and catching my breath. Apparently I exaggerated my breathing a little, which told the crowd how exhausted I was from all the effort, and that brought down a rain of laughter.

Somehow, that picked us up. We saw the humor in our feeble attempt to stay with this team. It was going to take all our energy just to stay alive, let alone try to keep the Bombers from scoring. And then I got an idea.

The Bombers were tired too. Not as tired as we were, of course, because defense takes more out of you. And they had bench strength, plenty of guys who could come in and give their front line a rest. But for that moment they were enjoying the break too.

82

The big guy, number 18, stood six feet from me, making no move on me or the puck. His chest was heaving. He was smiling at the little act between me and the crowd, and I knew that he knew that this game would not be a scoreless tie for long.

The Bombers were committed to the shutout, and one good way to accomplish that would be to get the puck back and keep it at our end. Eventually they would break through and score. And then again. And when we were totally exhausted, they would probably bury us. That was all right. We could see it coming. It was the way it should be. The fourth place team, a bunch of rookies from nowhere, had no business on the ice with these superstars.

But still, as I looked at the clock and the scoreboard, the game was still fresh, even if we weren't. The Bombers had not scored. Oh, they would. No doubt about that. But for those few delicious seconds, I controlled the puck at center ice, everyone was catching a breath, and we were not losing. Not yet.

I wondered if it would be possible, before the floodgates opened and the torrent of Bomber goals began, if we could surprise them and score first. It was wild, it was crazy. But why not? It would be a small victory. Something we would remember forever.

Let the people think what they wanted about me or my team. We were not cheats. And we weren't just clowns who fought the best we could and then comically stole a breather at center ice. I looked into the eyes of the Bomber defense. They looked lazy and fat. They knew they had us, and they enjoyed the break.

I toyed with the puck with my stick and looked at my teammates. I was hoping, wishing, longing, that I would see in their eyes the same idea I had. Could they not catch the idea and spring into action, while the Bombers were laying back, and just work a fast play that would sneak a goal into the net?

We didn't have to win. It was clear we wouldn't. But

couldn't we enjoy that little victory? Scoring first. Catching them off guard. Leading a team that would probably play for the state title.

I didn't even hope that if we pulled it off it would stun them or change their game plan or make them panic this early. I just wanted to do this so badly. But I was deeply disappointed to see that my teammates' eyes were hollow too.

Their faces were pale, their cheeks sunken. I knew I must look the same way. In fact, I tried to look more that way just to make my move even more surprising. All this was racing through my mind in the few seconds I controlled the puck at center ice.

And I knew I had to try. No one was in position to help, and they weren't thinking about goals. They were thinking about breathing and resting, and I couldn't blame them. I didn't want to be a hero, a solo act. I just had to try.

It would be my gift to my teammates. What a good bunch of guys they were! They had worked so hard, come so far, been so supportive of me when I did such an unpopular thing. Now I was committed to it. With one last look into the faces of my teammates and the opponents, I burst into action.

I switched the puck from one side to the other and drove directly at my opponent. His eyes grew wide as I juked at the last instant and slipped past him. His feet were together. He had not even started to push off.

No one else was moving! No one. I saw their goalie flinch, but by now I was across the blue line, charging at him with no teammate to help me and no defender in position to help him.

He was a good goalie and by now the element of surprise was gone. He would be ready. It would take the shot of a lifetime. From still a long way out I measured the shot, drew my stick back high on my left side, and cut loose.

My right skate dug into the ice as my stick blasted the puck and I followed through. The puck immediately jumped off the ice and whistled toward the goalie. My momentum carried me toward the goal, and I saw the horrible sight of the puck's rising. Its spin was causing it to sweep to the left.

He reached up too late as it sailed past his stretching form, over his glove. But it was too high! It caromed off the post and directly back at me. I was sweeping to the left myself and everything in me screamed to stop and turn and bat in the rebound, but I couldn't move fast enough.

The burst of a cheer from the crowd died as soon as it was born, and the puck banged off my hip. It bounced, the goalie tumbled to the ice from his effort, and somehow, some way, the puck leaked through the crease to the net.

The goalie sat dejected and swept it back out as the crowd screamed deafeningly. My teammates nearly knocked me down with their hugs and slaps. Even the Bombers seemed to have appreciated the effort, and a few called out. "Nice shot." "Nice going."

It was the last goal we scored. By the end of the first period we trailed 6-1. At the end of two 10-1. The final was 14-1. No other team scored on the Bombers in the tournament. They beat Pontiac 6-0 and then Carbondale 5-0 and 2-0 for the state championship.

We had earned our small victory and finished fourth in the state. And I had been able to present my teammates with a gift I hoped they would remember. I knew I would never forget it.